Ibrahim Khan

and the Mystery of the Haunted Lake

30180967994 77

For Abd al-Wakil and Maryam Azzam
Inspired by your love of scary stories

Ibrahim Khan

and the Mystery of the Haunted Lake

FARHEEN KHAN

THE ISLAMIC FOUNDATION

MUSLIM CHILDREN'S LIBRARY

THE IBRAHIM KHAN SERIES

Ibrahim Khan and the Mystery of the Haunted Lake
Author Farheen Khan
Editor Fatima D'Oyen
Illustrators Hisham and Sharelle Haqq
Cover/Book design & typeset Nasir Cadir
Coordinator Anwar Cara

Published by
THE ISLAMIC FOUNDATION
Markfield Conference Centre, Ratby Lane, Markfield
Leicestershire, LE67 9SY, United Kingdom
E-mail: publications@islamic-foundation.com
Website: www.islamic-foundation.com

Quran House, P.O. Box 30611, Nairobi, Kenya

P.M.B. 3193, Kano, Nigeria

Distributed by
Kube Publishing Ltd.
Tel: +44(01530) 249230, Fax: +44(01530) 249656
E-mail: info@kubepublishing.com
Website: www.kubepublishing.com

A Cataloguing-in-Publication Data record for this book is available from the British Library

ISBN 978-0-86037-423-7

CONTENTS

CHAPTER ONE

Triple Chocolate Delight

"Just open it!" yelled Zayn.

"Patience," whispered Ibrahim. "You have to do these things in the right order," he explained, as he sniffed the outside of the rectangular metal box. Carefully lifting it, Ibrahim weighed the box in one hand then the other, a skill he had picked up from all his detective work. After a few more minutes of careful consideration, he was ready.

"Spaghetti and meatballs!" Ibrahim announced.

"Are you sure?" asked Zayn.

"Positive," said Ibrahim. "Oh, and don't forget two… no three Triple Chocolate Delight cookies!"

Opening Ibrahim's lunch box, Zayn let out a yelp!

"How… how did you know?" Zayn stammered.

"Skill, my dear cousin, skill," replied Ibrahim, ruffling Zayn's already messy hair, which he liked to keep a little long.

Ibrahim, who was a little taller than his cousin, had short black hair and an infectious smile.

Pulling his lunch box towards him, Ibrahim took out the contents one at a time: a bottle of milk, a bag of grapes, three Triple Chocolate Delight cookies and, of course, a large container of spaghetti and meatballs.

"I wish I'd get a Triple Chocolate Delight cookie once in a while," Zayn complained, eyeing Ibrahim's snack. "All I ever get are apples, apples and more apples.

"My parents bought ten boxes – five from me and five from my sister – to help with the school fundraising drive. You're welcome to have as many as you like," Ibrahim offered.

"Really?" asked Zayn. "I'll be over right after school! Can you believe it? The class that sells the most wins a trip to Camp Chimo!"

"Yeah, that would be amazing," said Ibrahim. "Huda and her grade two friends set up a lemonade stand at our next door neighbour's garage sale last Saturday."

"That's really smart of your sister!" said Zayn.

Huda, who was just a year younger than Ibrahim, was a straight A student and head of the school book club. She always wore her long hair in a ponytail, covered in a long, colourful *hijab*.

"Come on Ibrahim, we're detectives and in grade three!" said Zayn "We should be able to come up with an even better idea to win this thing."

"I think the point is to raise money for schools in Eastern Nepal," reasoned Ibrahim. "The camping trip is just a way to get us excited."

"Well it's working," said Zayn. "Because I'm really excited!"

***

It was Friday morning, and all of Greenwood School was waiting for their principal to announce the winning class.

"I'm so nervous," said Zayn, sitting beside Ibrahim in the school gym.

"Relax," said Ibrahim. "We all worked hard and the money is going to kids who really need it. It doesn't really matter who wins."

"Of course it does!" said Zayn, looking indignant.

"Look! Here comes Principal Williams now," said Ibrahim.

Mr. Williams had wavy blonde hair with streaks of white. He was tall and had friendly blue eyes that turned a little darker whenever he got angry or upset.

"Sorry for the delay, children," said Mr. Williams. "I'd like to congratulate all of you for your effort in helping collect money to rebuild schools destroyed by fire in Eastern Nepal." A light clapping could be heard throughout the large gym. "Now, the announcement you've all been waiting for… The class that raised the most money is—Mrs. Morris' grade three students. Happy camping!"

This time the children clapped and cheered as loud as they could. The loudest of course, was the winning class.

"We did it!" yelled Zayn. "Camp Chimo, here we come!

CHAPTER TWO

Heading North

Mrs. Morris, a petite woman with long, straight brown hair, stood patiently in front of the class waiting for her students to calm down. She couldn't help smile at their excitement. They had worked hard to collect money for the needy, and she was proud of them. It was the end of the week and they'd be leaving for their three-day camping trip on Monday. All anyone wanted to talk about was Camp Chimo.

"What does 'Chimo' mean anyway?" asked David, who loved finding the meanings of new words and using them.

"Chimo means 'friend' and is used when saying hello or farewell. It was once widely used by the Inuit people here in northern Canada," explained Mrs. Morris. "The camp is situated on a beautiful conservation area just two hours north of here. It is on land that another native tribe, the Cree, once called their home."

"What does 'conservation' mean?" asked David, scribbling the word into a small notebook he always kept in his pocket. He wore thick glasses that were too big for his small face, and loved to read. David was also a senior member of Huda's book club.

A few children put up their hands.

"Yes, Ibrahim?" said Mrs. Morris.

"'Conservation' means people are not allowed to cut down the trees or disturb the animals and their habitats," he answered.

"Correct," said Mrs. Morris. "I expect you all to respect your surroundings while you're there. Your science teacher, Mr. Barnell, has kindly agreed to join us on Monday and will be staying with the boys in their cabin."

"Will you stay with us?" one of the girls asked nervously.

"Yes, Mariam," Mrs. Morris reassured her. "There's nothing to worry about."

"My brother said the lake is haunted," said George, with a mischievous look in his eyes.

George was older than the rest of the kids. He had missed a lot of school last year, and had been kept back in grade three because of his poor report card.

"Yeah, didn't he say the ghosts snatch you in the night?" said George's best friend Ali with a wink.

The boys sitting around George chuckled, earning them a glare from their teacher.

"Well, if there are no more questions, class dismissed! Don't forget to get your permission forms signed!" Mrs. Morris called after the loud children.

***

Monday morning came with brilliant sunshine. The large, yellow school bus stood waiting in front of the red brick building of Greenwood School. Mr.

Barnell's tall, lanky figure stood at the door of the bus, making sure no one forgot anything.

The excited campers piled into the bus, but no one immediately noticed who was missing. The Khan boys chose a seat near the front so that they could be the first ones out.

"Where's Mariam?" asked Zayn.

"She probably chickened out," yelled George, from two seats back.

"Maybe the ghosts got her before she could even get to the camp!" laughed Ali.

"That's not nice!" said Ibrahim. "She could just be late," but no one heard him over all the laughing.

A few moments later Mrs. Morris and Mr. Barnell boarded the bus.

"Okay guys, it looks like everyone who's coming is here," said Mr. Barnell, wiping his glasses and adjusting the sleeve of his brown tweed jacket.

Just as the bus door shut behind him, a loud horn filled the air.

"Stop, it's Mariam!" called Mrs. Morris.

A large black car swerved in behind the school bus. Mariam jumped out of the back seat with her

bag hanging off one shoulder. The back of her *hijab* billowed out behind her as she ran to the side of the bus. Just as she reached the door, her bag turned upside down and the contents spilled onto the sidewalk, including a small stuffed bear. This time no one could hold in their laughter. Even Mr. Barnell had a smile on his face as he came off the bus to help. Red-faced, Mariam finally got on and took a seat behind the Khan Boys.

"Okay," called Mr. Barnell. "Now that we're *all* here, let's go camping!"

The bus exploded in loud cheers.

CHAPTER THREE

Camp Chimo

"It's been two hours, seven minutes and 34 seconds, Mrs. Morris. Are we there yet?" asked Zayn. "I really need to use the washroom!"

"We're almost there," Mrs. Morris answered patiently for the eleventh time. "Please put your stopwatch away; it'll only make the time go slower."

"I was just trying to keep my *wudu*," Zayn grumbled to Ibrahim. "I guess I should have gone before we left.

"I guess you should have," said Ibrahim, turning another page of *The Adventures of Sherlock Holmes.*

Soon the bus began to slow down before pulling

over to the side of the road. The group had seen nothing but thick, lush forest for the past half hour, so it seemed like they were stopping in the middle of nowhere. A small, worn sign by the side of the road was the only distinguishable landmark.

"Is everything okay?" asked Ibrahim.

"Better than okay," replied Mr. Barnell. "We've arrived!"

The bus made a sharp right turn into a dirt road that led them straight into the forest. Branches loudly scratched against the top and sides of the bus as a cloud of dust rose up behind them. Coming to a stop in a large clearing, the group waited for the dust to settle.

"I just saw a ghost!" cried Ali.

"Not funny," said Mariam, crossing her arms.

"That's enough boys," said Mr. Barnell. "Stop teasing— Ghost!"

Everyone on the bus turned to see what their teacher was looking at. Several metres away from the bus stood a faint image of a man. It was as if a white glow surrounded him. All at once the bus erupted in loud, terrified screams.

"It's coming closer," yelled Zayn. "Someone do something!"

Soon another sound could be heard among all the screaming. It was Mr. Barnell, laughing so hard that tears were streaming down his cheeks.

"It—it's okay," he choked out, trying to calm the class. "Net—he's wearing a net!"

The children took a closer look at the shadowy man who now stood right outside the bus door. The ghostly figure had a friendly smile, as he waved at the children.

One by one the students tumbled out, looking embarrassed.

"Welcome to Camp Chimo!" said the friendly ghost, as he pulled off his netting. "I apologize for startling your class, Henry. I just finished removing a wasp nest that I found near one of our cabins, and this mosquito net was the only thing I could find to protect myself from being stung," he explained.

"Class," Mr. Barnell said, turning to his students, "Meet Mr. Parker, our guide for the next three days."

Mr. Parker had shoulder length black hair, which he kept tied with a black band, sparkling green eyes and a deep tan. He was tall and had broad shoulders.

"Hello, campers!" said Mr. Parker cheerfully.

The children mumbled greetings in return.

"Welcome to the only public camping ground within 75 miles of here," he said. "My family has been living in these parts for generations, helping to preserve and protect this beautiful land. Now, why don't you settle into your cabins? The girls' cabin is to the right and the boys' is just through the clearing on the left. For those of you who need to use the washrooms, there are toilets and showers in each cabin," he added, winking at Zayn. "We'll meet back at the meeting place by the fire pit in fifteen minutes."

The children grabbed their bags and quickly made their way to their assigned lodging. The log wood cabins were so deeply nestled between the trees they looked like tree houses. Each had fifteen bunk beds, enough to fit all the children. The wood floors were covered with well-worn rugs, while the floral curtains made the place look cozy. The smell of fresh earth and pine trees filled the air.

"*Subhan'Allah*, this place is beautiful," Ibrahim marvelled.

"Yeah, yeah, very nice," Zayn muttered, as he came out of their cabin washroom. "You know, I almost wet myself back there! That Mr. Parker guy really startled me."

"I think we were all startled," said Ibrahim. "That net and all the dust in the air really made him look ghostly! Try to relax. For once we're on a real vacation, with no mysteries to solve."

"You're right," said Zayn. "We had to eat a lot of Triple Chocolate Delight cookies to get here. We deserve a vacation!"

CHAPTER FOUR

The Legend of the Haunted Lake

That evening for dinner the children had a choice between beef barley stew and vegetable bean stew. The Khan boys got their vegetarian stew and found a spot on one of the outdoor picnic benches.

"*Bismillah*," said Zayn, starting to dig in. "Wow, I am really hungry. Mr. Parker said the cook is a professional from some fancy restaurant in town."

"Yeah, I guess you won't need all those snacks you bought with you," said Ibrahim.

"It never hurts to be prepared," reasoned Zayn.

"Prepared for what?" asked Ibrahim. "You could survive for more than a month with all that food!"

"Oh, gross!" said Zayn. "What is this brown, slimy stuff?"

"Probably just vegetables," said Ibrahim, taking his first bite. "Hmm, maybe Mr. Jones is better at meat dishes."

"Nope," said George, from the next table. "Looks like Pot-o-mush to me."

"Food is food," said Ibrahim. "Let's try to be grateful for what we have. Besides, it's possible this is just the way stew is made where Mr. Jones is from."

Once the children had eaten whatever they could of their dinner, they gathered around the large, roaring fire in the clearing. The fire pit served as the camp's meeting place, and was surrounded by a circle of logs for people to sit or lean on. Unlike the rest of the camp, the ground here was covered in soft sand.

"I hope you enjoyed Billy's hearty stew," said Mr. Parker. "I'll be trying my bowl a little later. Camp Chimo is very lucky to have a trained chef working for us. Mr. Jones left the big city life behind for the fresh mountain air. Isn't that right, Billy?"

"Yup," said Billy Jones, adjusting his apron. He had large hands and a friendly smile. His short, brown beard was speckled with grey. Around his neck he wore a small arrowhead on a string.

"Is that dirt under his nails?" Zayn whispered to Ibrahim. "Maybe that's why the food tasted so bad!"

"He was probably gardening or something," said Ibrahim, motioning his cousin to be quiet.

"Now, your teachers have put together scavenger hunt with a list of items for you to find during your stay here," said Mr. Parker.

"That's right," said Mr. Barnell, from his spot around the fire pit. "The first step is to figure out what the items are. You will have a list of clues, but will need to do some research to figure out what exactly you are supposed to find."

A collective groan could be heard among the children.

"You will be split up into four teams," their teacher continued, as if no one had made a sound. "There is a small library beside the kitchen, so I advise you to make good use of it. The first team to bring me all the items on their list wins!"

Once the students had been put into groups and had chosen their leaders, Mr. Barnell handed out the list of clues.

"'I change colour with the season, but am most red on my flag," read David, who was on the Khan boy's team. "I know that one!"

"Shh!" warned Zayn. "Don't give the answers away!"

"Yeah," laughed George. "No one else knows there's a maple leaf on the Canadian flag!"

"Some of the other ones aren't so easy," warned Mr. Barnell. "It would be wise to consult the library."

"Any questions before we say good night?" asked Mr. Parker.

"Why is this place called The Haunted Lake?" asked George. "My brother said it's a true story."

"Well, tell your brother he shouldn't believe everything he hears," said Mr. Parker. "Now, if there's nothing else I guess we'll call it a night. See you all in the morning. Breakfast is at 8.00."

With a wave to the children, Mr. Parker headed to his cabin.

"It's been a long day," said Mrs. Morris, with a yawn. "Everyone to your cabins, please."

"Would it be okay if the boys help me put out the fire," asked Billy, who had started to clear up for the night.

"Sure," agreed Mr. Barnell. "I'll see you boys back at the cabin."

The children began to scoop sand into a large bucket for Billy to pour over the fire.

As the girls, Mrs. Morris and Mr. Barnell headed to their cabins, Billy Jones turned to the boys.

"Do you want to know why they say this place is haunted?" he asked.

"Yes!" yelled Ali, before anyone else could reply.

"Well, have a seat then," said Billy, bringing his voice down to almost a whisper. "Long ago… almost 50 years ago today, there was a class camping here at Camp Chimo. It was a group of children much like yourselves. They had been over the rules and knew not to wander alone in the forest. But one young man, on a dare by his friends, decided to do something very foolish. At the stroke of midnight, as his friends looked on from the top of that very hill behind you, he walked to the lake below, got into a canoe and rowed out to the middle of the water. The full moon lit the entire forest, so he could clearly be seen by all those watching. However, instead of rowing back he just kept going. His friends who had gone out with him shouted out to him, but he was too far to hear. The next morning, when he had still not returned, search parties were sent out but the young man was never seen again. People assume that he drowned. Some folks say his ghost still visits this forest. If you listen closely, you might hear the paddle of his canoe rowing on the lake behind you!"

Instinctively all the boys turned to look down at the lake.

"Sleep well, boys," whispered Billy Jones, with a hint of a smile.

Both frightened and excited, the exhausted boys headed to bed.

CHAPTER FIVE

Early Morning Scare

"Zayn! Wake up," whispered Ibrahim. "It's *fajr*, get up!"

"Huh? How do you know?" asked Zayn, groggily. "It's so dark."

"I have all the *salah* times set on my watch," said Ibrahim. "Now hurry up and do *wudu* before you miss it!"

As Zayn shuffled to the bathroom, their classmates Ali and Yusuf plopped down beside Ibrahim.

"How are we going to figure out what direction to pray?" asked Yusuf.

"I have just the thing," said Ibrahim, rummaging through his bag.

"You brought your brown sack with you?" asked Ali. "I thought you guys only used that when you're on a case."

"Well, you never know when you might need it," said Ibrahim, pulling out a small compass.

Once they were done praying, the boys decided to sit on the small front porch of their cabin. The sky was still dark grey, and the morning fog hung thickly in the air. Suddenly the boys heard a soft moaning coming from the trees.

"What animal is that?" asked Ali. "I don't think I've heard it before."

"That's not an animal," said Ibrahim, getting up. "Zayn, grab some binoculars from the sack. There's something out there."

Before Zayn had a chance to go in, the moaning became even louder. Then, from behind a group of low bushes, rose a white billowing figure. It floated in the air for what seemed like several long minutes before disappearing.

The frightened boys stood for a moment, staring at the spot they had seen the figure before they all ran back into the cabin.

"It's the ghost of that boy Mr. Jones told us about!" shouted Ali.

"Except it didn't look like a boy anymore!" yelled Yusuf.

"That moaning was so creepy, I still have goose bumps!" said Zayn.

"What boy? What moaning?" asked Mr. Barnell, who had just woken up and had no idea what was going on. "Would you boys please keep it down? Ibrahim, can you please tell me what's going on?"

"Well, sir," said Ibrahim, trying to gather his thoughts. "As Muslims, we know there's no such thing as ghosts, but there *is* something strange going on."

All four boys took turns recounting the story they'd heard the night before, and what they saw and heard this morning. The more they talked about it, the less frightened they felt.

"Let's just keep this between us for now," advised Mr. Barnell. "I don't want the other children getting scared. If you see anything else, let me know."

The boys agreed to keep their eyes open and their mouths closed, but before the end of the day, somehow almost everyone had heard of the incident.

***

"So, does this mean that Ali and I are detectives too?" asked Yusuf at breakfast that morning.

"Sure, you guys can be our assistants," said Ibrahim, carefully eyeing Ali, who was sitting at the next table with George. "I just hope this isn't one of George's practical jokes. Ali and George are good friends."

The table fell silent as the promised breakfast of 'hot oatmeal and wild berry surprise' was passed around.

"This actually wouldn't be that bad if the burnt smell wasn't so strong," said Zayn, licking his spoon.

"*Alhamdulillah,* it's good to see you eating something other than those sugary snacks you brought," said Ibrahim.

"Yeah, but I hope Mr. Jones learns his way around the kitchen soon," said Zayn, looking worried. "I'm already running low!"

Banging a ladle to a pot, Mr. Parker got the attention of all the diners.

"Today's activities include canoeing, fishing and swimming, but I would suggest you get started on your scavenger hunt if you hope to win."

"I'm sure the Khan boys will get right to work," laughed George. "We wouldn't want to have any fun, would we?"

Zayn just scowled at George, but Ibrahim was smiling.

"That's not a bad idea," said Ibrahim to his group. "We could be done with our list before anyone else gets started."

"Oh, come on!" groaned Zayn. "Canoeing looks like so much fun."

"It'll be even more fun when our work is done," said Ibrahim.

"What do you guys think?" Zayn asked the other team members, who were sitting at the table with them. To his dismay, everyone agreed with Ibrahim.

CHAPTER SIX

Scavenger Hunt

"Zayn, would you please get to work?" Ibrahim asked his cousin for the fourth time that morning. "Mariam, Yusuf, David and I are all looking up our items. You need to work as part of the team."

"Okay, okay," said Zayn, reluctantly getting off his chair in the dimly lit library. The library was actually a cabin, similar to other cabins at Camp Chimo, but instead of being full of beds, bookshelves lined the walls, filled from end to end with dusty books. In the middle of the room was a round wooden table, surrounded by worn leather chairs. There were several lamps around the room, but heavy curtains prevented the natural light from coming through the windows.

"I wonder if we'll find any arrowheads?" Zayn mumbled to himself, making his way to where the others sat.

"Finally," said Ibrahim, when he saw that his cousin had opened a book at last. " 'The Mystery of the Haunted Lake?'" asked Ibrahim, when he noticed the title. "Zayn, you're supposed to be solving your scavenger hunt riddle, not reading ghost stories!"

"No listen," said Zayn. "It says here—"

"I don't want to hear what it says," Ibrahim snapped. "The rest of us have figured out our items and are ready to go canoeing. When you're done, you are more than welcome to join us."

Surprised by his cousin's outburst, Zayn simply stared as the rest of his team walked out the door, leaving him to read his ghost story and finish his work.

✶✶✶

That afternoon's lunch was a very bright green 'Pot-o-mush,' and both the vegetarian and meat options were suspiciously similar looking. Though the Khan boys sat together, neither one spoke to the other.

"Are you sure this stuff is even food?" Zayn asked Yusuf, making sure Ibrahim knew he was ignoring him. "I can't tell if it's animal, vegetable or mineral!"

"Well, it's approved as part of our vegetarian meals so it can't be animal," said Ibrahim, with a smile. "I'm sorry for yelling at you, Zayn," he apologized. "You were in that library all morning. I should have come back and helped you."

"I forgive you," said Zayn, smiling back. "You know I could never stay mad at you for long. It actually didn't take me that long to figure out what my item was, but I did find some interesting reading material."

"Zayn Khan reading on vacation," Ibrahim laughed. "That'll be the day! Now, come on guys, let's finish our lunch so we can splash around in the lake."

"I think I've had all I can eat," said Yusuf. "When is Billy going to make something edible? I'm already running low on Halal Hassan's Marshmallow Treats."

"You brought Halal Hassan Treats?" yelped Zayn. "And this is the first I'm hearing of it?"

"I thought you brought your own snacks!" said Yusuf.

"I'm on my last few," said Zayn. "I'm going to need to restock soon!"

"However did you convince your parents to give you all that junk food?" asked Ibrahim.

"I think they were just sad I'd be gone for so long," said Zayn. "Also, I was supposed to share with everyone else, but with all these food disasters, it's all I have to survive!"

"It is a little odd that a trained chef would make as many mistakes as Mr. Jones has," said Ibrahim. "I guess it takes time getting used to a new kitchen."

As the boys cleared their table, they didn't notice the figure standing in the shadows of a nearby pine tree, listening in on their conversation.

CHAPTER SEVEN

Another Morning Scare

After *fajr* the next morning, the Khan boys found themselves back on the front porch of their cabin. Yusuf and Ali had gone back to bed after saying their prayers, to catch up on some more sleep before breakfast.

"Do you think we'll see anything unusual?" asked Zayn.

"I hope so," said Ibrahim.

"Yusuf and Ali are pretty scared," said Zayn.

"I know," said Ibrahim. "I'm starting to think George has nothing to do with this."

Once the early sunlight began to filter through the trees, Zayn grew impatient.

"Let's wake up Yusuf again and go down to the lake," he suggested. "I have to catch a fish for my scavenger hunt item."

"Your scavenger hunt item is a fish?" asked Ibrahim, in disbelief.

"Yeah, why? What's yours?" said Zayn.

"'A smooth, hard, flattened sphere, found by a lake, a beach or a pier,'" said Ibrahim, pulling a small grey pebble out of his pocket.

"Well, mine is a fish," said Zayn, getting up to grab some fishing poles.

Reluctantly, a sleepy Yusuf agreed to join them.

"It's only 5.30! We don't need to be up until 7.00," he said. Looking down the hill, he added, "Doesn't the lake look creepy with the fog hanging over it?" rubbing his hands together for warmth.

"I think it looks cool," said Zayn. "Like the Sherlock Holmes mysteries Ibrahim's reading all the time."

Getting into the canoe, Ibrahim slowly rowed out to the middle of the lake. Zayn, who had put some bait at the end of his fishing rod, tossed his line out.

"It really is peaceful out here," said Ibrahim. "It's nice to not be scared of this 'ghost' fellow. We know *Allah* is our Protector."

Not five minutes had passed when the boys heard a familiar moaning sound, along with splashing noises by the shore they had just left.

"What's that?" asked Yusuf, panicking.

"I see something," said Zayn, squinting thought the mist. The thick fog made it difficult to see the shore.

"Careful, guys," warned Ibrahim. "You're rocking the boat."

"It's the ghost!" yelled Yusuf, quickly standing up. The sudden motion made the canoe flip over with a loud splash, landing all three boys in the cold water. Yelling and screaming, the boys finally made it to shore.

"Where—Where'd he go?" asked Yusuf, out of breath.

Instead of a ghost, the boys found Mrs. Morris, Mr. Barnell and Billy Jones staring down at them.

"What in the world do you boys think you're doing?" asked Mrs. Morris, with her hands firmly on her hips. "It is 6 o'clock in the morning!"

"I—we—," Yusuf tried to explain.

"We were trying to catch my scavenger hunt item," said Zayn.

"But we saw something– that thing that's been pretending to be a ghost," said Ibrahim. "We panicked and tipped over the canoe."

"Scavenger hunt item?" asked Mr. Barnell. "What were you looking for in the middle of the lake?"

"The fish!" said Zayn. "You know, the thing with overlapping scales that's open when dry and closed when wet."

"That's a pinecone!" said Ibrahim, Mr. Barnell and Yusuf, all at the same time.

"Oh…" said Zayn. "Sorry."

"Well it *is* the best time of day to catch fish," said Billy Jones, who was laughing so hard his belly shook. "You boys had better get into some dry clothes before you catch a cold."

Before the group left the water's edge, they heard more splashing.

"Who's there?" asked Mrs. Morris.

"Hello," said Mr. Parker, coming out of the water in his swimsuit. "Are you boys enjoying a cool morning swim, too?" he asked. "You might want to try it without the jeans next time; it'll help you float better," he chuckled.

Grabbing his towel, Mr. Parker wrapped it around his waist and headed in the direction of the camp.

CHAPTER EIGHT

Moonlight Hike

"Why would Mr. Parker want to scare off visitors?" asked Zayn, munching on some blackberries from a nearby bush.

"It doesn't make sense," said Ibrahim. "Unfortunately, he's on top of my list of suspects."

"Who else is on it?" asked Yusuf, who had been taking his job as assistant detective very seriously.

"It's a short list," said Ibrahim, biting his lip in frustration.

Ibrahim and Zayn had been to the areas where the ghost had been seen, but they hadn't found any clues. The forest floor near their cabins was covered mostly with loose pebbles and pine needles, which didn't seem to have been disturbed, and the sandy beach at the lake's edge had too many footprints to make any sense of them. It was the afternoon of their second day at camp. Most of the children were swimming in the lake or canoeing on it. Ibrahim, Zayn and Yusuf were sitting close to the water under the shade of a large, black walnut tree.

"How does the ghost know we'll be out there?" asked Yusuf. "We keep seeing him right after *fajr*. If *we* weren't awake, no one would have seen it."

"And if no one had seen it, there'd be no one to spread fear to the rest of the campers," reasoned Ibrahim.

"Guys," said Zayn. "I think we're being played."

"By someone who has access to information about us," said Ibrahim. "The forms our parents filled out when we registered had our prayer schedule, along with our vegetarian meal requests!"

✳✳✳

A moonlight hike though the forest was planned for that evening. As the children gathered around, Mr. Parker arranged them all in a line.

"This will make it easier to move along the narrow trail. Remember who's behind you and who's in front of you," he advised. "I'll lead, while Henry will make sure no one's left behind."

The children, who were a little nervous about going into the forest at night, moved a little closer to one another.

"It's a special treat to be here during the full moon," said Mr. Parker. "It's a spectacular sight. If we don't make too much noise, we might be able to see some of the nocturnal creatures that live here."

It wasn't long before the kids forgot their fears and began to enjoy their surroundings.

"Look up," said Mr. Parker. "There's a male Snowy Owl. Unlike the female, they are almost completely white. On some nights it looks like a ghost is flying around."

The children laughed nervously as they followed their guide.

"Look! A flying squirrel," said Mr. Barnell, from the back of the line. "Notice the wing-like membrane of skin that extends between their wrists and ankles. They don't actually fly, but glide from tree to tree."

The time flew by, as the students whispered and pointed to the night creatures. Mariam almost stepped on the tail of a black-footed ferret, but Kathy's grabbed her arm just in time.

"Those were once believed to be extinct," explained Mr. Barnell. "In 1986 a small group of eighteen was discovered. A lot of work has been done to help increase the black-footed ferret population. Now there are around 750 in North America!"

Coming to a small clearing in the woods, Mr. Parker turned to the group.

"Let's take a five minute break before we head back," he announced. "I'm just going to fill my water bottle from a stream up ahead. It's truly the best water you've ever tasted."

The children sat in a small circle as they waited for their guide to return.

"Could a wild animal attack us out here?" asked Zayn. "Those ferrets had some pretty sharp claws."

"We're a large group," said Mr. Barnell. "I'm sure we'll be fine."

But as soon as those words left his mouth, they heard the familiar loud moaning from deep in the forest.

"G—Ghost!" yelled George, even before he saw one.

"Ghost!!" yelled all the kids.

Everyone ran in a different direction. Mr. Parker, who had just stepped back into the clearing, tried his best to help Mr. Barnell calm everyone, but no one could hear them over all the panic and yelling. Fearing the children wouldn't be able to find their way back, Mr. Parker and Mr. Barnell built a fire in the clearing, hoping it would help to guide the students. After a half hour only fifteen of the twenty campers had returned; five were still missing.

"Alright, campers, let's put out this fire and head back to camp," said Mr. Parker.

"But what about the rest?" asked Mariam, fearfully looking into the dark forest. "We can't just leave them out there!"

"I'm hoping they've found each other and are already back at the camp, waiting for us," he reassured her.

CHAPTER NINE

Ghost!

Zayn, who had panicked at the sound of the ghost, grabbed Ibrahim's sleeve, dropped it again and barrelled into the forest. Only after several minutes of running did he slow down enough for Ibrahim to draw near. Before Ibrahim could get mad at Zayn for running, the boys heard a loud, hollow laugh coming through the trees.

Grabbing Zayn's arm, Ibrahim pulled him to the ground.

"Follow me," Ibrahim whispered, slowly crawling towards the noise.

As they got closer they noticed the dying embers of a small campfire from behind a camouflaged camping tent. The shadow of two men could clearly be seen. One was an averaged sized man with a round belly, who looked oddly familiar. The other was much taller and bald, with broad shoulders.

"I think we really scared them, Stan," said the shorter man, whose voice the boys immediately recognized as Billy Jones'.

"Did you see those brats run?" laughed Stan. "Once news gets out that the ghost of the Haunted Lake has returned, this place will be deserted."

"Finally we'll be able to dig this place up without worrying about nosy campers hanging around," said Billy Jones, with a chuckle.

"What happened to those kid detectives you were worried about?" asked Stan.

"I've been keeping a close eye on them," said Billy. "I'm pretty sure they're convinced Parker's behind the whole thing!"

Ibrahim crawled closer, trying to sneak a peek at the taller man, but Zayn grabbed his foot, motioning his cousin not to go any further.

"I just want to get a quick look at Stan," Ibrahim whispered. "Then we'll go back to camp and get help."

"It's too dangerous!" said Zayn, a little too loudly.

"Hey, who's there?" yelled Billy. "Circle around, Stan; I think someone's in the bushes!"

Ibrahim and Zayn's eyes grew wide; they knew there was nowhere to run. Lifting the back of the tent, Ibrahim shoved Zayn in, then squeezed in behind him. The small tent had an old rumpled sleeping bag on the ground and a small wooden crate, splattered with mud.

"We're trapped," Zayn mouthed.

"I know," whispered Ibrahim, silently praying for a miracle.

The boys watched in horror as Stan's shadow drew closer to the back of the tent where they had just entered from. Suddenly, they heard a loud shout from the forest behind them.

"Aaaahhhh! Run for your lives!" It was George!

"Let's scare him off!" said Billy.

The two men took off into the forest after George.

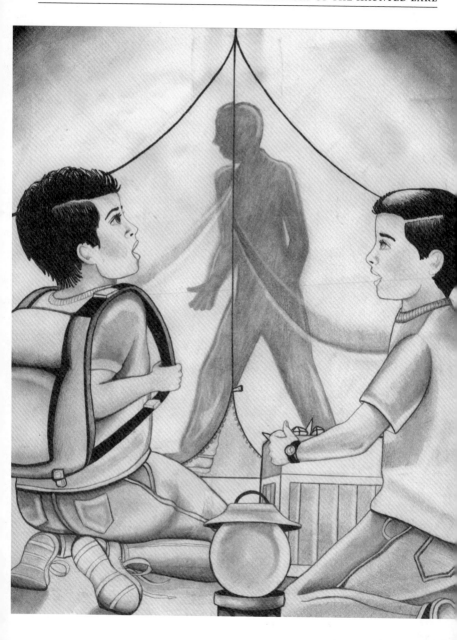

"Is that boy still screaming from back in the clearing?" asked Zayn in amazement, rummaging through the muddy box.

"It sounds like it," smiled Ibrahim. "I don't think he's in any danger though. According to my compass, George is heading straight towards the camp. I don't think our 'ghost' wants to turn up there with Billy. Now is our chance to get away."

"Look at this," said Zayn, holding up an ancient looking, ivory-coloured arrowhead. "It looks just like the one Mr. Jones wears around his neck! And there are some more things in here – beaded jewellery and stuff."

Let's take the arrowhead with us," said Ibrahim. "I read that some native tribes made them from antlers. We can examine it on our way back."

CHAPTER TEN

Captured

"Wasn't the book you were reading in the library called 'The Haunted Lake'?" Ibrahim asked as they hiked back to camp.

"Yup," said Zayn, pushing branches aside with a long stick. "It had the same story Mr. Jones told us on our first night here. It also had a map of this area, showing an ancient burial site for the Cree Indians on the other side of the lake."

"That's probably what the men are trying to dig up," said Ibrahim. "I'm sure there are private collectors who would pay a lot of money for ancient artefacts."

"Not just artefacts," said Zayn. "Apparently the Cree people were the largest tribe in the area and one of the most important. According to the book, some gold and silver may be buried there. The only reason it's been safe for this long are people like Mr. Parker and his family."

"What do you know about his family?" asked Ibrahim.

"The book I was reading was written by John Parker," said Zayn. "The author's father was British and his mother was a full-blooded Cree Indian. My guess is that John Parker is somehow related to *our* Mr. Parker."

"That's some great detective work!" said Ibrahim, stepping into the clearing of Camp Chimo.

Everyone, including Mr. Barnell, George and Billy Jones, was back, and had gathered around the meeting place.

"Where do you think Stan is?" asked Zayn.

"Probably back at his camp," guessed Ibrahim. "When we tell everyone what's happened, we'll have to keep Billy out of it for now."

"Why?" asked Zayn, but before Ibrahim could answer, Mrs. Morris came running over to the boys.

"There you are!" she said, looking relieved. "We were all so worried about the two of you."

"We're okay," said Ibrahim. "And we found out who's been trying to scare us."

Ibrahim and Zayn took turns telling everyone what had happened. They were careful to leave Billy's name out of it, making Stan the only culprit. Mrs. Morris called the police while Mr. Barnell, Mr. Parker and the Khan Boys got ready to head back into the forest.

"I'll come with you," said Billy. "You might need me."

"Sure," agreed Mr. Parker. "We might need an extra hand out there."

The boys led the small group back to Stan's camp.

"You boys wait back here," said Mr. Barnell. "If anything goes wrong, run back to camp and bring the police here."

Ibrahim and Zayn hid behind a thick maple tree while the adults approached the campsite.

"Let me talk to him first," offered Billy. "I'll tell him the game's over. Hopefully he'll come with us peacefully."

There was no sign of Stan outside the tent, so Billy entered the tent through the front while Mr. Barnell and Mr. Parker stayed outside, in case he tried to run.

"What if Billy and Stan try to take down Mr. Parker and Mr. Barnell?" asked Zayn.

"If I'm right, Billy doesn't think he's a suspect," said Ibrahim. "I think he'll try to convince Stan to surrender rather than risk himself being caught."

Within minutes Billy brought out a tall, bald man with his hands tied behind his back.

CHAPTER ELEVEN

Heroes

The police had just arrived when the group stepped back into the clearing.

"We've been looking for this guy for a long time," said the sergeant. "He's wanted in several provinces for disturbing native burial grounds and removing artefacts belonging to local tribes."

"You boys are heroes," said Mr. Parker.

"You know," said the sergeant. "I always thought there were two of them. Seems like a lot of work for one man."

Making sure Billy was still close by, Ibrahim turned to the officer.

"There *is* more than one," he said. "There's a reason Camp Chimo's cook can't cook."

Everyone turned to Billy as his eyes widened in fear. He turned to make a run for it, but Mr. Barnell put out his foot. With a loud thud, Billy landed face first in a pile of fresh mud.

***

"Why didn't you tell me Billy was involved?" asked Mr. Parker.

"Billy was always around when the ghostly moans were heard," explained Ibrahim. "Zayn and I only heard him talking to Stan, so we had no proof. We needed him to prove his own guilt by running."

As Billy was being taken away in handcuffs, he turned to Ibrahim.

"How did you know it was me?" he asked with a scowl.

"A simple process of elimination," said Ibrahim. "Well, that and your cooking!"

The class clapped and cheered as Billy and Stan were taken away.

"You know," said Zayn, turning to Mr. Parker. "At first we thought it was you."

"I guess I was always gone at the wrong time," he laughed.

"But we couldn't figure out a motive," said Ibrahim. "Especially after Zayn read the Haunted Lake book."

"So, you found my grandfather's book in the library," said Mr. Parker.

"You have a very rich family history," said Zayn, yawning. "You should make it part of the Camp Chimo experience."

"Not a bad idea," said Mr. Parker, smiling. "Now, go get some sleep! It's very late, and I'm afraid breakfast tomorrow will be cold cereal with milk."

The children hollered and cheered!

CHAPTER TWELVE

The Last Day

The children thoroughly enjoyed their last day at Camp Chimo. Ibrahim's team was the only one that had successfully completed the scavenger hunt. They won a return trip to the camp with their families.

"That really is the best news ever," said Zayn, dipping his fingers from the side of the canoe into the cool water.

"Yeah," agreed Ibrahim. "Huda will love it here, especially after working so hard trying to raise money."

"I'm glad we worked on the scavenger hunt instead of canoeing," said Zayn. "I'm already excited about coming back here!"

"You deserve it," said Ibrahim. "If it wasn't for your research, Billy Jones would have continued to feed people that awful Pot-o-Mush."

"You're right," said Zayn. "I never thought of it that way. I probably saved hundreds of people from terrible food! They should name a cabin after me—"

"Don't let it get to your head," said Ibrahim, laughing. "You know it was *Allah* who guided us to catch those guys."

"—and then they should put up a plaque!" said Zayn, with a faraway look in his eyes, too busy with his own thoughts to hear what Ibrahim was saying.

Ibrahim did the only thing he could think of to make his cousin stop. He stood up in their canoe, tipping it over—again!

Glossary

Alhamdulillah
'Praise be to Allah (God)'

Allah
God Almighty

Astaghfirullah
'I seek Allah's forgiveness'

Bismillah
'In the name of Allah'

Fajr
Prayer before sunrise; one of the five daily prayers

Halal
Food prepared according to Islamic guidelines

Hijab
Headscarf

Salah
Ritual prayer, offered five times a day

Subhan'Allah
'Glory be to Allah'

Wudu
Washing the face, head, hands and feet before prayers

Word Search

Can you find the following words hidden in the grid on page 72?

- Ali
- Arrowhead
- Artefact
- Billy Jones
- Brown sack
- Camp Chimo
- Canoe
- Conservation
- Cree
- David
- Ghost
- Haunted Lake
- Ibrahim
- Khan boys
- Mr Barnell
- Mr Parker
- Mrs Morris
- Yusuf
- Zayn

I	E	E	L	F	Y	H	M	B	U	E	D	N	V	D
J	G	O	U	V	E	D	R	Q	S	U	W	O	A	A
D	Z	S	N	A	S	O	B	L	K	W	F	I	E	E
K	U	A	L	A	W	T	A	N	R	Z	A	T	Q	H
Y	H	I	Y	N	C	R	R	S	C	E	O	A	X	W
C	O	A	S	N	T	R	N	L	K	O	W	V	D	O
I	A	A	N	E	E	H	E	A	I	O	M	R	X	R
D	C	M	F	B	I	L	L	Y	J	O	N	E	S	R
K	E	A	P	Q	O	D	L	N	I	T	S	S	F	A
R	C	W	J	C	E	Y	G	H	O	S	T	N	J	C
T	D	I	V	T	H	Q	S	N	J	A	P	O	N	C
A	I	D	N	J	M	I	H	A	R	B	I	C	J	C
X	V	U	M	N	T	P	M	R	P	A	R	K	E	R
G	A	A	U	S	I	R	R	O	M	S	R	M	Z	E
H	D	Z	N	N	M	Q	E	F	V	N	A	M	V	E